ISBN:

E-book: 979-8-9893168-6-1

Paperback: 979-8-9893168-5-4

Edited By: Shelby Goodwin

Cover Designer: Coffin Print Designs

For those waiting to find their Thorne

AUTHOR'S NOTE

This book contains elements of:

- Death of a loved one (off page)
- Explicit sexual scene
- Strained family relationship
- Fantasy war mentions

Please make sure you are protecting your mental health. If you need more information send me a message on any of my socials. Otherwise, happy reading!

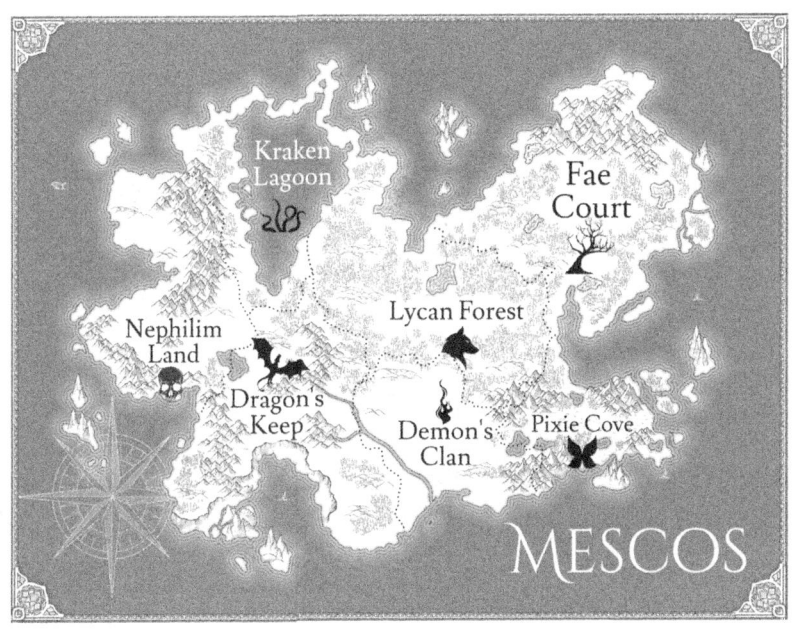

CHAPTER 1

TALLIE

The smokey aroma of bacon fills the air. The scrambled eggs in the pan have just reached the right consistency when the front door opens. Before they have a chance to burn, I take the eggs off the heat and whirl around to greet my visitors.

The King Alpha fills the doorway, chestnut-colored eyes scanning the room. When they land on me, his features soften and a small smile plays on his lips. It's not a real smile; I know my cousin too well, but it's something. As children, Rip was carefree and adventurous. However, since taking over as the pack's leader, he was forced to change.

I miss the man he used to be, but I'm proud of the man he became for our pack.

"Just in time for breakfast," he hums.

"Almost as if you planned it that way." I sneak a smile. "Luckily for you, I made way more than mom and I can eat."

"Enough to feed two more mouths?" he asks.

"Two?"

My cousin steps inside my home. His massive size makes my already small house feel like it's bursting at the seams. But I don't dwell on that fact for long, because behind him I catch a glimpse of umber-colored skin. My breath hitches as my cousin's second, Alpha Thorne, enters my home.

Like my cousin Rip, Thorne is shirtless. Most males, and some females, tend to walk around with little clothing so shifting to our wolves is easier.

Thorne wears his jeans low on his hips, giving a tease of what I know to be a rather impressive length. My cheeks redden at my wayward thoughts, bowing my head in his direction. "Alpha Thorne."

"Beta Tallie," Thorne greets, his voice reminding me of sweet, warm honey.

I hate how formal our interactions in public are, but I have no one to blame but myself. And honestly, I don't know how we've kept it a secret for so long. I suppose with the threat of the Nephilim in our borders, most of the pack and Rip's attention have been elsewhere.

"Of course I have enough. Please, join us." The crack of bacon grease behind me pulls my attention away, and I quickly scoop out the last remaining pieces and place them on a paper towel to pat off the excess grease.

"Where's Aunt Imelda?" Rip already has a plate piled high with food. He reaches past me to grab the bacon. I don't stop him because I doubt he's eaten in the last twenty-four hours judging by his unshaven stubble and the dark circles underneath his eyes.

Him and his inner circle have had many late nights—

quite a few of those late nights left me without seeing Thorne for days on end. Little of their discussions is known to me, but their meetings started when the rogues started attacking more consistently.

"She's getting dressed. I'm sure she will be down here soon," I say.

Rip takes his plate of eggs, bacon, toast, and pancakes to the table. With his back turned toward us, Thorne takes the opportunity to walk behind me and reach for a clean plate. In the process, his chest presses into my back and his free hand lingers close to my hip. I feel every hard muscle of Thorne and my body flushes with heat.

Pictures of his rough hands roaming my body makes me shiver. He has made me come undone time and time again because those hands know exactly where to touch me. The whisper of a touch he's giving me now is almost cruel. A tease of what I can't have. At least not right now.

All too soon, Thorne moves away from me, and I mourn the absence of his heat. "Thank you for breakfast." He winks at me, dishing up the last of his scrambled eggs, before joining my cousin at the table.

I soon join them, my plate half the size of theirs. Thorne's eyes follow me as I take the seat next to him, keeping our chairs at a respectable distance. Rip doesn't notice or care where I sit, because he makes no objection.

"So, are you here to talk about the mating ceremony?" I ask after a moment of comfortable silence. My mother has been our mistress of ceremonies ever since Rip and I were small children. She ran the biannual mating ceremonies and celebrations of life and death within our pack. She's damn good at it too, planning everything down to the smallest of details.

It's a job I hope to inherit when my mother retires. Knowing her though, it will be a while yet. Still, I have fun helping her plan each event while learning all of her tips and tricks.

"Yeah," Rip says between bites. "Need to know how many newly mated couples we have."

"Oh, I know. We have five couples." I smile. I looked over those names at least two dozen times and memorized every one on that list. More notably, I recognized who is not on the list.

Rip curses under his breath. "Damn, that's more than I thought."

My brow furrows and I glance at Thorne who refuses to meet my gaze. Clearly he doesn't like what my cousin has planned, but before I can ask Rip what he means, my mother barges into the room, black curls bouncing with each step.

"Rip, good morning my sweet boy." My mother places a kiss on top of the King Alpha's head and I swear his cheeks flush. It doesn't matter that her "sweet boy" is the king of our pack because to her he will always be the timid little boy who lost his parents at a young age. Until he moved into the Alpha Estate, he lived with us.

"Auntie, you look beautiful today," he says in a way of greeting.

And she does. My mom holds on to her youth; only a few wrinkles around her eyes hint at her age. She wears her beautiful curly hair down her back. I love when she lets me braid it. Even as a little girl, I was enthralled with playing with my mother's hair.

Her dress is a simple blue color, and not one I've seen before.

"Is that from Velma's store?" I ask about the sweet, omega woman who supplies most of the clothes in Lycan Forest. She's been our main source for clothing for longer than I've been alive.

"It is, and I picked you up a few things too, my darling." My mom flutters over to me now, kissing the top of my head. For just a moment, I'm a little girl again and nothing in my life is complicated.

The illusion shatters when Rip asks, "do you have a moment to talk, Auntie?"

I let my mom go, and she follows Rip into the other room. I had hoped they would have their conversation in here, but Rip likes to keep me in the dark about a lot of things. He has dubbed himself my fierce protector and tries very hard to keep me out of danger.

Unfortunately, that also means he keeps me uninformed.

The only silver lining is that I'm finally alone with Thorne for the first time in days, but I can't even enjoy it because curiosity gets the best of me.

"Why does Rip want to talk about the mating ceremony with my mom?"

Thorne is not a good liar, which is why it amazes me that Rip hasn't caught on to our secret relationship. Indecision paints his expression, and I reach for his hand, threading our fingers together. I angle my body closer to his, leaning over to show off my ample cleavage.

I'm not playing fair, but I'm not certain I care.

Apparently neither is he, because instead of answering my question, Thorne leans forward and presses his lips to mine.

Everything else melts away.

CHAPTER 2
THORNE

When Rip said he needed to go over to his Aunt Imelda's house, I quickly offered to go with him. If he was suspicious of my eagerness to volunteer, Rip didn't show it. These days he is far too in his own head to read the people around him.

I don't blame him. Not with the impending threat coming to Lycan Forest. Hard decisions are going to have to be made, and Rip's on his way to make one now.

Tallie, my sweet beta, is going to be upset.

Alphas hate being too far away from their partners. Especially those of us who are unbonded because we are unable to know if they are safe.

It's fucking painful.

I want to claim her. To let others know Tallie is mine. My wolf grows agitated the more days that go by where we haven't mated her yet.

I do my best to keep my emotions in check when we arrive at Imelda and Tallie's house, but already I can smell the citrusy scent of My Star.

When we arrive, Tallie doesn't notice me at first, giving me time to admire her. Today she's in a light yellow dress that makes her golden eyes pop. Her tawny skin is on full display for me and I yearn to run my hands over every inch of that beautiful, brown body.

When Tallie finally sees me, I can't help the slight smirk that crosses my lips. Her breath hitches and her chest rises and falls as if she had just finished running a mile.

Having her this close and not being able to touch her is a testament to my ability to resist temptation.

Because that is Tallie: a delicious temptation.

When Rip announces he needs to speak with Imelda in private about the upcoming mating ceremony, the confusion and an undercurrent of fear in Tallie's expression means questions will come as soon as we are alone.

Questions she's not going to like the answer to—so I do the only thing I know to keep her quiet.

I kiss her.

Her scent envelopes me and I growl. I pull her close until Tallie is seated in my lap. The rational part of my brain knows this is a bad idea because anyone could walk in on us at any time, but I'm too far gone to care.

I run my hand through her thick, curly hair, wrapping it around my fist. I tug her head back and Tallie moans. My Star likes a little pain with her pleasure.

I pry her mouth open with my tongue and she relents to my will. I taste her like this might be the last time I ever taste her. That any moment could be our last, so I make every kiss with her matter.

"Alpha," she moans, arching her back toward me. Her scent floods my senses and I groan. She smells like a citrus tree, reminding me of the middle of summer, my favorite time of year.

"Yes, My Star?" I break the kiss, but then I trail my lips down her exposed neck. She shudders. Her hard nipples poke through her dress, demanding my mouth on them.

Soon, I promise myself.

"Rip could walk in." Even as she says this, her hands move down my body to the obvious bulge in my pants. Her gentle fingers glide over my cock and I want nothing more than to fuck that pretty mouth of hers.

"He could," I agree, gently nipping at her neck where my mating mark should be.

"And you are trying to distract me—ah!" The breath leaves her lips as I move my hands from her soft hair to grip her ass.

We are walking a dangerous line here, but I'm not certain I care.

"Thorne, we can't." Her words are laced with sadness and I pause. That is all she needs to push away from me, creating space between us. Tallie bites her lip and it does little to extinguish the blazing fire within me.

My fault, of course. I started it.

I don't regret it though.

"Please, Thorne. I need to know what he's talking to my mom about. It has to be important, whatever it is, or he wouldn't bother coming over."

She's right, but I'm not ready for the disappointment

and sadness in her features when I tell her why we're here.

She must sense my trepidation because she offers me a soft smile. "Please, my love. Let me see how I can help."

And since I can't deny her, I speak the words she isn't going to like to hear.

CHAPTER 3
TALLIE

Thorne sighs. "Things aren't good, My Star."

"What do you mean? Are there more rogue attacks?" There's been an increase of attacks as of late, which is why Thorne is constantly called away since he's Rip's second. But is there more?

"Yes, but something else too," his eyes flicker close and I can see for the first time just how drained he truly is. Instant guilt washes over me because how can I claim to love this man and not know what demons he's facing?

I pray they aren't *actual* demons because we've held a peace treaty with the demons for decades.

"We got word from King Malix in Dragon's Keep. They recently had an attack on their land from the Nephilim. Gadreel broke free of his prison and King Malix believes we will be their next target."

All the air in my lungs leaves my body and fear like I've never felt before tries to consume me. The Nephilim. The Nephilim have escaped and their leader is free once again.

The Nephilim are ancient creatures from nightmares. Giants with shredded wings, hellbent on destroying everything around them for power and the ability to rule our land.

Long ago, the seven leaders of Mescos managed to imprison every last one, but not before they cursed our kingdoms. In one hundred years if our leaders don't find their human mates, misery and death would befall our lands.

It seems like an easy enough task, but the portal between our realm and the human realm was destroyed in battle. No one has access to cross between...at least no one that I know.

"But...why would this affect the mating ceremony?" My brain can only focus on that one thing. The only thing I have a marginal amount of control over. Panic and worry start to form as questions arise about the fate of our pack.

"Because Rip believes it could prove to be too dangerous. That the rogues or Nephilim may attack when our guard is down. Tallie, listen—"

Thorne rarely uses my name in private. It is always "my star" or "my love." Never Tallie unless he's under a lot of stress. Is my strong alpha...scared?

"Don't go into the woods. Never leave the house without an escort. I would prefer it if you never left the house, but I know that's not realistic."

"It's not realistic at all. Not for me or anyone. This is only going to give birth to fear." Fear isn't a natural emotion to wolves. Prolonged exposure would only weaken us and make it all the more easier for the Nephilim and rogues to pick us off one by one.

"If anything, we should move up the mating ceremony," I say. "It will strengthen our pack, like it does every year. We can't deny the mates their right at a proper ritual, Thorne. We can't."

I don't remember standing, but suddenly I'm pushing my chair back. Thorne reaches out, bracketing my wrist with his large hand. "Tallie, you need to think rationally here. I know this is a sensitive topic for you because—"

"Don't say it." I've never been mad at Thorne, never felt the need to run away from him, but right now I want nothing more than to be far away. Far away from the pitiful looks I receive. Thorne has never once pitied me, but today, his eyes tell a different story.

And I can't handle it.

I pull away from my alpha. Thorne is bigger and more powerful than me, so if he wanted to, he could force me to stay back.

But he doesn't. He lets me go.

It's a small reprieve, but a reprieve nonetheless.

I turn my back on my alpha, and storm out of the kitchen, leaving my breakfast plate mostly untouched.

Thorne is the easy obstacle. My cousin is another entity entirely.

But I refuse to back down and let him deny mates their right to mating.

Just as he has done to me before.

CHAPTER 4
THORNE

I don't always like being an alpha.

Alphas have to make hard decisions for their pack in order to keep them safe. Sometimes we have to make others unhappy, even if they don't realize it is for their own protection.

To everyone else, Tallie's reaction might seem extreme, but I know why she lashes out at me. This mating ceremony weighs heavily on her, even if she won't talk about it with me or anyone else in the pack. I wish she had someone she could confide in, but ever since the incident, Tallie has pulled back and retreated into herself.

She's protecting her heart and pride.

I get that on a fundamental level, but instinctually I wants to pull her back to the table and command her to stay until the threat to our kind passes, no matter how long that takes.

Except, if I do that, Tallie would hate me. I can't have My Star look at me any other way than with love.

Tallie storms out of the room, but I'm only steps behind her. Her curly brown hair hits my chest and hints of cinnamon waft up from her shampoo. Her scent intoxicates me and it becomes hard to concentrate on anything other than the way her hips sway and the roundness of her ass.

Get your shit together, Thorne.

Both Imelda and Rip's attention are drawn to Tallie's fiery spirit. Rip narrows his eyes. Our King Alpha has been under a lot of stress with the news coming out of Dragon's Keep and the curse plaguing their lands. It's only a matter of time before Lycan Forest is shown the same fate.

So, his patience runs thin these days. Another reason why Tallie and I have not approached him for our mating blessing.

"Darling, what is it? Something wrong?" Imelda attempts to reach for her daughter, but Tallie ignores her outstretched arms and walks straight to Rip.

"What do you mean you are canceling the mating ceremony? You can't do that Rip! We've been planning this for months!"

If anyone else spoke to the King Alpha like Tallie is, he'd have their tongue for it. Rip isn't a cruel leader, but he is our pack alpha and has to set examples. Luckily, he's always had a soft spot for both Tallie and Imelda.

"Tallie, this doesn't concern you."

"Oh, please," Tallie rolls her eyes. Does the beta not understand she's on thin ice? Even Rip has breaking points and she is about to find his limits.

My instinct is to protect her. To draw her away from

Rip and hold her behind me, but that's not possible for me to do at the moment. And that fucking kills me.

"You always say that," she continues, "You treat me like a delicate flower and never let me help. And as your cousin who has you and our pack's best interest in mind, I think canceling the mating ceremony is a terrible idea. Our pack looks forward to it and it strengthens us. Why would you deny us that?"

Rip's jaw ticks, but that's the only indication of his anger. Like most of his emotions, he keeps his feelings hidden.

"I deny the pack nothing. This is for everyone's safety."

"Bullshit!"

"Tallie!" Imelda gasps horrified. "Enough, child. You do not speak to our alpha like that."

"Perhaps, but I do speak to my cousin Rip like this." Tallie holds her ground, cousin against cousin. The room grows tense, as if it too can sense Tallie is playing with fire.

The cousins are locked into an intense stare down with one another, both unwilling to break eye contact. Tallie puts up a valiant fight, but she soon succumbs to her alpha's stare and looks away, backing up into her mother's arms. Her brown cheeks flush red.

"Sorry, Alpha, I just..."

"Don't."

Tallie's head snaps up, confusion written across her face. "Don't what?"

"Titles. Not in private. We're family, Tallie. That has never changed."

"Rip, then," she starts again, a small smile playing at her full lips. "Please don't cancel the mating ceremony. We need it. The pack needs it. And each newly mated couple has gotten your permission. You're a man of your word, are you not? Keep your blessing to them."

Rip lets out a deep breath. At this moment, he appears older than his twenty-six years. As far as alphas go, he's the youngest we've had in centuries. That much responsibility on any one's shoulders will age a man before their time.

"This is something important to you," Rip says after a moment.

"Yes very, but not just to me. It's important to those newly mated."

She's not wrong. The ceremony solidifies the bond between the couple, connecting them in a way that merges their soul as one. For alphas, it heightens our abilities and makes us aware of our partners through the mate bond.

It's a big deal to the pack, and Rip knew this going in. His decision is not going to be a popular one, especially to the alphas and betas with omega mates. Omegas aren't safe until partnered with their alpha.

"Do you know who the mated wolves at the ceremony will be?" Rip asks, a concerned tremor in his voice.

My blood boils. I know why he asks, but I don't like it. I don't like it because of a particular male participating in the ceremony. To think of another male with my Tallie enrages me to my core. Despite my best efforts, a low growl leaves my throat.

Tallie's golden eyes meet mine. Her eyes gloss over,

but before any tears can fall, she blinks them away and nods to her cousin. "Yes, I'm aware Alpha Daven will be part of the ceremony."

"Then you also know that he is mating Omega Lillian?" Rip asks and Tallie nods, not meeting his eyes. Despite their relationship ending abruptly three years ago, hurt and anger linger inside her.

Rip must also sense her sadness because he places a soft hand under her chin, tilting her face up to him. "Denying your request to mate Alpha Daven was hard for me, but I do not regret it. You understand why I denied your request, don't you?"

"I do now." Her voice comes out as a whisper. The rational part of my brain knows she's no longer in love with Daven, but the animal side of me wants nothing more than to rip the other alpha in half. My wolf grows unsteady.

"Alphas tend to take omegas as mates and I didn't want you to be hurt when Alpha Daven found his omega. Because he would have. I saw the way he looked at Omega Lillian while you were dating. I wanted to spare you life-long heartache, even if I had to hurt you in the process."

"But not all alphas need omegas. There's several happily mated alphas and betas," Tallie reiterates. My body tenses and I send thanks to our goddesses that Rip isn't paying me any mind. I would give away our relationship in a second if he was.

"I'm not saying it's impossible, and betas and alphas can be happy together, but I know the alphas in my pack. Most of them will end up with omegas because that's just biology, Tallie. This is why I said I will only approve your mate if they are a beta."

"But—"

"Enough." Rip holds up his hand to silence her. Tallie clamps her mouth shut, but there's a storm brewing inside of her. "If it is so important to you, we will keep the ceremony, with obvious safety changes. I expect you to help your mother with the planning and to stay away from my alphas."

Tallie looks like she wants to argue again, but her mother speaks up first. "We will make sure this ceremony is both safe and special for our new mates. Won't we, Tallie?"

"Sure," she mutters before spinning on her heels and heading straight past me and out of the room.

She got what she wanted, but at a cost.

"I'll make sure she's okay," Imelda says after a moment of silence. "You know Tallie, she gets over things quickly." She plants a kiss on Rip's cheek before following after her daughter. Imelda squeezes my shoulder in a kind gesture as she passes.

Only Rip and I remain.

"We should go. We have new safety protocols to discuss." Rip looks no happier than Tallie did only seconds ago. Each cousin is hurting, but for different reasons. I know why My Star hurts, but Rip is still a mystery to me, even though he's my best friend.

Wordlessly, I follow him out.

Leaving Tallie behind once again.

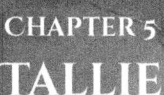

I scrub at the already clean plate, my body working on autopilot.

I just walked away from the King Alpha. If I were anyone else, I'd be punished for my insubordination. But I'm not anyone else; I'm Rip's younger cousin. Rip, who is like a brother to me and wants what's best for me.

Rationally, I know that. I used to be fine going along with what he said since it was Rip, and I looked up to him in so many ways.

But who I mate has never been something either of us have agreed upon.

When wolves find their mates, before they are allowed to go through the ceremony, they must get their blessing from their King Alpha. I've heard stories of King Alphas long ago who denied mates simply because they could. The mates never lived much longer after the refusal, dying from what we can only describe as a broken heart.

Rip is not like the cruel alphas from the past. He has yet to deny anyone their right to a mating ceremony... anyone except me, that is.

Which is completely embarrassing.

Shortly after it happened, the word had gotten out and I found myself the talk of the pack. I hated the attention and the pitiful glances. Poor Tallie, her own cousin wouldn't allow her to marry the alpha she claimed to love.

What is even worse is that Rip was right about Alpha Daven. I didn't want to admit it then, but I had been a lovestruck girl, intoxicated by her first true romance that I didn't see the signs. Not until after we were denied our mating ritual.

Alpha Daven had been rejected by two omegas previously. Omegas have an uncanny ability to determine the character of a person. They knew immediately that Daven is good at wearing masks, pretending to be the person you so desperately want him to be.

Since he had been rejected by omegas, I was his next target and I fell for his pretty lies and colorful deceit.

But, I'm not a foolish girl anymore. I guarded my heart for years afterward, afraid to let anyone in close, out of fear it would end in humiliation and heartbreak. Hell, I was determined to remain unmated for the rest of my life and simply be the best auntie to Rip's future children once he found his mate.

Then plans changed.

And sometimes love can blossom in the most unexpected ways.

I first met Thorne as a young girl, shortly after Rip's

parents died. He had stayed by my cousin's side during their funeral, and the two formed a strong bond. It was to no ones surprise that when Rip was crowned as King Alpha, he chose Thorne as his second.

I'm not sure when our feelings of friendship soon turned to something more, but I do remember the night I kissed him.

Rip had left to check in on the construction of the new nursery in town. Thorne and I found ourselves together and a free night for him is a rarity. We spent it together, under the stars and around the fire, making s'mores. The evening had been perfect.

Thorne had been perfect.

He made me hopeful for the first time in ages. I don't know what came over me that night, but I was the one to make the first move. I kissed him, right by the fire. His body tensed under mine and I immediately thought I made a mistake and backed away. I didn't get far before he pulled me back and kissed me like a starving man, desperate for his next meal.

It was the start of our story, but unfortunately it hasn't progressed much since then. We steal secret moments, hoping time will slow for the night so we don't have to go back into the real world.

I'm far too lost in my own misery to hear my mother approach until she's standing behind me, placing a hand on my shoulder. I jump, dropping the pan below me into the soapy water.

"Oh, I'm sorry darling. I thought you heard me come in. Here, let me take that." She takes the wet towel from my hand and pushes me aside. "These dishes are already clean, honey. They didn't stand a chance against you," she jokes, but it falls flat.

"Okay, are you ready to talk about it or should we pretend like what just happened didn't happen?"

"That option. The last one," I murmur.

Mom juts her hip out, a hand resting on it as she gives me the *"oh, we are most certainly talking about this,"* face, and I have no other option but to speak.

"I guess I'm just sensitive about the whole mating ritual." Which isn't a lie, but it's also not the entire truth. It's a safe answer, and my mother knows it.

"Mhm," she says, knowing I'm full of shit. "Take a seat, Tallie."

"I'm fine—"

"Sit your ass down, girl."

I sit my ass down at the kitchen table.

She smiles, humor shining in her eyes. "So, let's try this again. Let's talk about what happened between you and Rip. Your cousin loves you, you know. He's only over-protective because he wants the best for you."

I do my best not to roll my eyes. The thing is, I already *know* that. I've never once doubted Rip's love for me, even after he denied me a mating ritual with Daven. But I'm not a child he needs to look after like when we were kids.

"Don't you think I want what's best for me too, mom? That I want to find happiness like everyone else?"

"I want that for you too. I know you told me you were okay with being alone, but an unmated life is not a life a young wolf should strive for. I would not change my time I had with your father for anything. Those were the happiest moments of my life and I got the best daughter out of it."

Mom crosses the room and plops down in the seat next to me, her eyes shiny with unshed tears. She always tears up when talking about my father, her late mate who passed away five years ago due to a rare shifter disease.

"I want that for you, honey. And I think you do too, no matter how much you claim you don't." Then she pulls me into her arms and hugs me.

There's something about being in your mother's arms that transports you back to your childhood. I'm no longer a twenty-four year old woman, but a five year old child afraid of the dark. The dam I have so meticulously built over the past few years begins to crack and I burst.

Emotions I've hid for so long pour out of me and once they start, I can't stop them. Sobs wrack through my body and my mom does her best to console me, her hand running up and down my back soothingly. Just like she did when I was a child.

I'm not sure how long we sit here. Minutes. Hours. She doesn't ask me to speak; not that I could anyway. She holds me, and it's exactly what I need right now.

Finally, the sobs reside and I'm left feeling hollow. My body is drained, purged of emotions and I feel like I could sleep for days.

"I need to tell you something, mom," I murmur, pulling out of her embrace.

"Are you finally going to tell me about him?" She asks and my heart stops.

"You...know?" I tried so hard to keep it a secret. I

thought I kept it a secret, but perhaps we had been reckless. If my mother knows...then who else knows?

Reading the panic on my face, my mom offers me a smile. She wipes away the few stray tears on my cheeks. "I had my suspicions. After your reaction to Rip, it all but confirmed them. Plus, I'm your mother. There are very few things you can do that I don't know about. So, are you ready to talk about it?"

"I'm in love, mom." The words fly out of my mouth, desperate for someone—anyone—to hear them. For so long I've been screaming into a void with no response and now I have someone who knows.

It's...refreshing. And slightly terrifying.

My mom's face lights up like a child on christmas. "I knew it! For the last few weeks you've been coming home from the nursery with the biggest smiles on your face. I know you love the pack pups, but this was different. This was him, wasn't it? Tell me, who is it?"

"Alpha Thorne."

Her smile drops and my heart along with it. I expected this reaction, which is why I kept it secret for so long, but it still hurts all the same. "Say something. Please. Anything."

"My girl," my mom starts, reaching for my hand and giving it a gentle squeeze. "Alpha Thorne is a fine wolf. Handsome and kind. He'd make a good mate. But, are you willing to *share him* if he finds his omega?"

"He won't," I say with more certainty than I feel. "He loves me and only me. He's never believed in alphas only dating omegas. His own parents are an alpha and a beta pairing and are one of the strongest couples in our pack.

It's possible, momma. You have to want it enough, and we do. We want this."

I wait for her to tell me I'm delusional. That I'm falling into the same trap I fell into with Daven.

But she doesn't say any of those things. Instead, she leans forward and says, "I can think of no one better to love you than Thorne. Now, how will we convince Rip of this?"

CHAPTER 6

TALLIE

The crisp winter air kisses my skin, causing my wolf to purr inside me. This is her favorite time to run, feeling the cold air through her fur. It's been a week since I last shifted and I'm desperate to shift soon. I've been so busy with preparations that I haven't had the time for much else. Plus my secret meetings with Thorne take up most of my time.

I clutch the basket in my hands a little tighter, smiling to myself. My cheeks hurt from the amount of smiling I've done today.

When I finally told my mom about Thorne, everything poured out. I told her about our meetings together and the future we planned. How my relationship with Thorne feels different from anything I have experienced in the past.

There's a change in me.

And it's because I found my mate. I know it is.

Rip will see in time.

After my conversation with my mom and helping her

with a few more details for the ceremony next week, she helped me make a surprise dinner for Thorne. I had not planned on seeing him tonight, but my mom promised she'd keep Rip busy, giving us time alone.

His home is not located too far from mine, just a mile on the other side of town. I pull my coat tighter around me. It's late, so few people will be out wandering the streets. Still, I want to be careful.

The dimly lit dirt road that leads to Thorne's house is empty, save for an older beta couple sitting on their front porch, smiling at one another. They're completely oblivious to the world around them.

I want that.

I want that so badly.

I move quietly past them, but neither beta pays me much mind. Thorne's house is only feet away.

Like most homes in Lycan Forest, his house is built entirely out of wood, giving off a cozy, warm charm. His home is one story, but spacious with two decently-sized bedrooms. The beautiful kitchen has enough storage to stay stocked up through the winter, but his living room is my favorite part of his house.

Thorne is good with his hands, in more ways than one, and builds all of his own furniture. It's uniquely Thorne, and that makes me love it all the more. A large, wood-burning fireplace is the focus of the room. We have spent hours snuggled together or making love by the flames.

My cheeks flush when I approach his front door. I knock, taking a step back to wait for him. Anticipation builds, but it soon deflates after a moment when no one comes to the door.

I frown. He has to be home. His lights are on and my mom is with Rip, so he's not conducting business right now.

I reach for the knob and it turns in my grip. Unlocked. My confusion only heightens as I open the door and step through the threshold.

A blazing fire burns from the fireplace, heating the room to a comfortable temperature. I place my basket of food down and take my coat off, placing it neatly on the couch.

An open book lay on the coffee table with a half-drunk cup of coffee next to it. Thorne's coat hangs on the rack, next to a smaller, unfamiliar coat.

"Thorne?" I call, but get no response.

Disappointment starts to seep in at the realization that Thorne isn't home.

Of course he's not home. You didn't tell him you'd be coming over, I chide myself.

Realizing this is a lost cause, I reach for my coat but stop abruptly when I hear a laugh.

A feminine laugh.

The hairs on the back of my neck stand up and I follow the sound of the voice. I tell myself there is a logical explanation as to why another female is in Thorne's house, but my heart isn't too keen on believing it.

I stay to the shadows, walking down the hallway leading to Thorne's kitchen. The voices grow louder and I hear the familiar deep voice I've come to love, laughing at something his guest said.

My heart sinks to the bottom of my stomach as I peek around the corner, praying to our goddesses I'm not about to see what my mind is picturing.

It's no use though.

Standing with his back to me, Thorne leans against the counter holding a glass with what looks to be wine in it. The woman is obstructed by Thorne's tall frame, but even from here I can smell her sweet scent.

An omega.

But not one I've seen before. The woman has dark red hair and pale skin that reminds me of fresh snow. She's small; smaller than me by at least four inches. Like most omegas she appears delicate and meek.

My brain is still trying to process what it's seeing when the omega leans in and hugs my alpha. Vitriolic anger like I've never experienced before courses through my body, lighting up every sense. My wolf rages inside, needing to claim her mate.

Mine. Don't touch!

A low growl leaves my lips, alerting the omega and Thorne to my presence. The omega is the first to notice me. Her small mouth forms a perfect "O," and she at least has the decency to look ashamed. Scared even.

She takes a few steps away from Thorne, her wide eyes scanning the room as if looking for the best places to run and hide.

The muscles in Thorne's back tighten and he's slow to turn around. The raging anger I felt not moments ago burns out, leaving nothing but embers and emptiness in its wake.

This is not happening again.

This *can't* happen again.

For a moment, neither Thorne nor I speak. I don't think I can form words right now if I tried. He looks like a man who has just been found with his hand in the cookie jar. Guilt and another emotion I can't quite figure out color his features.

And then he steps in front of the omega. Shielding her.

From *me.*

Something fundamental breaks inside of me. My heart, which Thorne meticulously pieced back together, shatters again. This time, I'm not certain there's coming back from this darkness creeping in.

"Tallie, *wait!*"

But I don't. Thorne's command echoes in the room, but I'm already running out of the house, past the front gate and down the vacant street.

Then I let my wolf rip free from her cage.

CHAPTER 7
THORNE

Fuck!

That could have gone a lot better. I hadn't expected Tallie to show up. She always warns me before she comes over. How long had she even been here and why didn't I notice her?

Well, I know why. Omega scents overpower those of betas, so unless you are paying attention, you won't smell a beta. Plus this new omega is so frail and scared. My concentration was on helping her feel comfortable and letting her know she is safe here.

"Did I get you in trouble?" A meek voice asks from the corner of the room. Omega Zora sits, huddled in a corner, trying to make herself small.

"It wasn't your fault." I try to keep my voice as neutral as possible. The last thing I need is a distressed omega and my runaway beta. "I need to go check on her. I'll lock the door. Don't open it for anyone, omega. I have a key. Do you understand?"

The omega nods, though the poor girl is terrified out

of her mind. Having me out of the house may calm her nerves, since she is skittish around alphas right now. She wouldn't go near Rip. Out of the two of us, I was the most approachable.

"Yes, alpha," she replies and I attempt a smile. It feels more like a grimace, but it makes Zora relax.

"Help yourself to anything in the house. The guest room has fresh linen," I say as an afterthought. I don't wait for her to reply; in a matter of seconds, I'm across the room and out the door. It locks behind me.

Her scent lingers, but it's faint and I can't track her for long. I make it to the end of the road, but that's when her scent vanishes. Below me are human footprints, but those soon turn to those of a wolf. And they head straight for the forest.

My stomach drops.

And my wolf rips out of me. *Mate. Find her,* he growls, incensed that our mate could be in danger and we are the reason for it.

I'm familiar with the forest, having done patrols nearly every night. I know what dangers lay in wait for their next victim. If not the rogues, then the dangerous terrain.

The night is getting colder, near freezing. Tallie can't survive in the immense cold with no provisions. There's been talk of snow too, which means my window for finding her is closing rapidly.

I howl, the sound reverberating around the trees, back to me. Nothing meets my response, not even the chirping of crickets. I'm utterly and completely alone.

So where the fuck is Tallie?

Her tracks are faint and frantic. I trace her steps deeper and deeper into the forest and dread begins to build, but I push it aside.

I can't lose focus now. Tallie needs me, so I push myself harder and harder, urging my legs to carry me faster.

I don't know how long I run, trying to escape the ticking time bomb looming over my head. Each second that ticks by puts Tallie in more danger. Twigs and thorns scratch my body, but I barely notice. My focus is on My Star.

I'll never get the look of betrayal out of my mind for as long as I live. She thinks I betrayed her. That I chose someone else over her, as if anyone else could make me feel even marginally as good as her. I've made many mistakes in my life, but my biggest one is not claiming her publicly, consequences be damned.

If—no, when—I find her, I'll make this right.

Tallie's tracks end abruptly as if she had vanished into thin air. Fear like I've never known it before grips me as my mind conjures up the horrible things that could have happened.

The ground here is damp, easy to slip if you weren't careful. Broken branches and mud add to the danger. I peer closer, seeing something in the mud, markings of some sort. It's as if something—or someone—lost their balance and slipped down the rather sharp incline, leading down to another part of the forest.

Then, that's when I hear it.

A small whimper. Barely audible, but there.

I try to catch a glance down the hill, but it is too dark,

even for my wolf eyes. Another whimper carries up from the darkness, followed by a moan of pain.

Tallie!

My wolf is desperate to get to her and howls. There's a small ledge I can jump down to below, and I hope that provides me better visibility. With a running start, I jump off, landing about ten feet below me.

I scramble to right myself before falling below, but from here I have a better view of this part of the forest. Sharp rocks cover most of the surface below me, along with a small stream. Or what might have once been a stream. The water is low and tiny pebbles line the bottom.

Movement to my right catches my attention. Gray fur peeks out between a boulder and a dead tree.

I'm still so high up, but I don't see any other way to down other than jumping. The fall isn't going to kill me, it won't even injure me much, but it'll sting like hell. I push off with my hind legs and then I'm free falling only seconds before I hit the ground with a loud *thud.*

The breath is knocked out of my lungs, but the adrenaline coursing through my body has me up in seconds, sprinting to the place I saw Tallie's wolf. The scent of blood fills the air and when I get close, I notice the awkward angle of her back foot.

Broken, for sure.

When I'm by her side, I shift. The icy winds slice through my body as I fall to my knees next to her. Tallie's eyes are closed and there is a dark patch of blood behind her ear. I'm the furthest thing from a healer, but I think the blood is just a nasty surface cut, nothing life threatening. It's her leg that concerns me.

I reach out gently to run my hand over Tallie's fur. Her wolf whimpers and opens one eye. "My Star, I need you to shift. I need to see where you're hurt." I keep my voice light and soft, so as to not spook her.

Tallie doesn't respond at first, but then she shifts. Naked and cold, she curls into herself and it's like a punch to the fucking gut.

"Oh, my love..." I whisper, stroking her cheek. She jerks away from me but winces. My eyes scan the rest of her naked body, looking for other injuries, until I get to her right foot. It's purple and most definitely broken. She's not going to be able to put weight on it. At least not without putting herself through a lot of pain, as well as slowing us down.

"Sweet girl, I'm going to have to pick you up, okay? Don't fight me, Tallie. Let me carry you back home to a healer."

She nods almost imperceptibly and a breath of relief leaves my lips. I slide my hands underneath her petite body. This time she doesn't flinch away. She moves into my arms as I pull her to my chest. She leans her head against me, reaching up to wrap her arms around my neck.

"Good girl." I stand with her in my arms, surveying the territory around us. Off in the distance, I hear the steady stream of water. Using that, I can navigate us home, though I'm not sure how long it'll take us. I'm afraid it's the only option I have right now since she can't climb back up the hill.

"I'm taking you home," I whisper, listening to the steady beats of her heart. Tallie's breathing evens out and I realize she's fallen asleep. She shivers close to me and I wish I had a blanket to wrap her up in.

I tuck Tallie in close to my chest and run. Though she's light, running through the forest as a man and not a wolf without my heightened senses isn't an easy endeavor. Perhaps this is my punishment. It's what I deserve.

I ignore the pine needles stabbing my feet and the rough bark of trees as I pass them. I shield Tallie from the worst of it, taking more than one branch to the face, but soon the lamplights from town glow in the distance.

I push forward the last mile, only slightly winded from the treacherous journey back. It's late, so the streets are free of curious eyes, which thankfully allows me to walk without being harassed.

We walk past the healer's cabin. There's no light or smoke coming from inside, meaning that I'll have to rouse one of the healers out of sleep. No matter, but I need to get Tallie home first. Her house is close. I see the light shining through the windows and two silhouettes.

Imelda and Rip.

Knowing I can no longer put off the inevitable, I carry Tallie home, opening their front door. Two sets of eyes swivel to meet mine, various levels of disbelief on their faces.

Then all hell breaks loose.

CHAPTER 8
THORNE

"**W**hat the fuck happened?" Rip is in front of me, trying to take Tallie. I hold her tighter, growling at him. I've never been one to push Rip's button, but I feel feral and ready to rip out the throats of anyone who tries to take her away from me.

"Stand down, Alpha." Rip glowers, his eyes shine a deep gold. It's a warning; telling me that his wolf is close to the surface, but so is mine. One wrong move will set us both off. I try to remain calm since I still have Tallie in my arms.

"She needs a healer." I push past my King Alpha and walk over to Imelda. Turning my back on an angry alpha is not only foolish, but deadly. Rip is in his rights to attack me, but I'm banking on the fact that he won't because I'm holding his cousin.

"Imelda, she needs a healer," I say, my voice gentle with the beta, even though inside I'm raging.

Imelda doesn't reply. She looks at her daughter and

her eyes fill with tears. She's lost a mate already and her daughter is all she has. I don't believe Tallie's injuries are life threatening, but I won't rest easy until Tallie is properly checked over by a healer.

"I'll go get Thomas," Imelda says, frantically running to the door. Thomas is their neighbor and one of the town's healers. She's gone before I have the chance to thank her.

"Thorne," a low, gravely voice comes from behind me. "What the fuck happened?" Each word is grit through his teeth with barely contained anger. His alpha command makes me falter, but nothing is going to stop me from putting Tallie down in her bed for the healer to assess.

"Thorne—"

"I'll tell you everything, Rip," I growl, more venom in my voice than I've ever used with him. Or for anyone for that matter. Rip's not only my best friend, but my King Alpha. Speaking to a King Alpha like this should get me punished.

And it probably would if I wasn't Rip's second. I'm not sure if my position will help me when I finally tell him the truth.

Rip simmers behind me, but lets me go. I fully expect his ire later. Tallie moans in my arms, eyes fluttering. She's going in and out of consciousness and I hurry to her room. Rip has to open the door, but I barrel inside and place her on top of the covers.

Not a moment too soon because Imelda and Thomas run in after me. Thomas appears hastily dressed, as if

Imelda dragged him out of bed herself. Since it's the middle of the night, she probably did.

Imelda flops a bag onto the bedside table and Thomas searches through it, pulling out two vials. A pale lavender-colored liquid encapsulates one of the vials. It's a healing tonic, one I know all too well. The healers keep them well stocked because it provides relief to their patients. The other vial is filled with a pale pink cream.

"When did you find Beta Tallie?" Thomas asks, assessing my mate. It takes everything in me not to snap at him to hurry up.

"Not too long ago. About ten minutes. I brought her straight here." Thomas doesn't respond as he continues to assess Tallie. Rip pulls Imelda into her arms, comforting his aunt as she looks on to her daughter with fear and sadness.

All because of me. It's my fault.

"Seems like you found her quickly," Thomas comments. His able fingers trail over her body. I know it's to check for injury, but I still let out a warning growl. Both Thomas and Imelda glance in my direction.

"Calm, Alpha. He's doing his job," Imelda's sweet voice says. For her sake, I try to stay calm.

Thomas continues his assessment, confirming what I already knew. A broken leg. There's not much he can do, but bandage her up and make sure she's comfortable. "She should be fine in a few days. Just make sure she remains in bed."

"We will. Thank you so much Thomas. I'm sorry I had to call for you at this hour," she says.

"Think nothing of it. Though if you want to apologize, your famous carrot cake would be the way to do it."

Despite the tense situation, Thomas's words make Imelda smile. It brightens up the otherwise dark mood of the room.

But only for a minute.

Rip hovers at Tallie's door, his eyes fixed on me. We lock gazes and for the first time, I feel true fear over what Rip will do or say. He has the power to keep Tallie and I apart. I hope it doesn't come to that, but I have to prepare for that reality. Prepare myself to fight my best friend because there is no way I'm leaving my mate.

Imelda must sense the growing tension between me and her nephew because she says, "I'm going to walk Thomas home. Then I can check on the Omega at your house, Thorne. Make sure she's okay before I come back."

Due to the excitement from the evening, I almost forgot about Omega Zora awaiting her mate at my house.

I nod my thanks, unable to form any words. Still, she understands and gently squeezes my shoulder before going over to Rip and doing the same to him. "I'll be back soon. Please don't upset my daughter more by hurting Thorne."

I don't hear what Rip says in reply because I'm not paying attention to them. I move to Tallie's side, tucking her stray hair behind her ear. Knowing there's no more secrets, I bend down and press the softest of kisses to her temple.

"Thorne," Rip growls from the doorway. "Come."

Knowing I can't put off the inevitable for much longer, I leave Tallie's room. As much as I want to stay with her, I know Rip wouldn't allow it. He wants answers and I'm ready to give them.

We walk in silence out of Tallie's room and down the hallway. It's not until we reach the main room of the house does Rip turn to face me. "How long?"

"A little over a year," I reply and he curses.

"What the fuck, Thorne? My fucking cousin? You can have anyone in the damn pack and yet you chose to break the heart of my cousin?" Rip's anger is misplaced. He's still so certain that I will take an omega.

It's true that alphas tend to gravitate toward omega mates. Breaking the hearts of betas is a common occurrence here, but that's not always how the story goes.

It's not how *our* story goes.

"Tallie owns my heart. Just as I own hers. You think I would destroy the most beautiful and perfect thing in my life just because an Omega walks across my path?"

"I'm not saying you'll do it on purpose. I'm saying it's a possibility," he retorts.

Rip has always protected Tallie, even to her detriment. I understand needing to protect the ones you love, but he can't dictate her life forever.

"And it's a possibility that an omega will see another alpha and leave their current relationship. Or see a beta and want to make a life with them. What I'm trying to say is it could happen in any relationship. That's the risk of giving your heart away, knowing it's only safe for however long the other person wishes to carry it.

"Your way of thinking, brother, is dated and rooted in toxic traditionalism that simply doesn't exist anymore," I say and Rip stiffens.

I sigh and take a step forward. "King Alpha, I love your cousin. I have loved her for over a year and I want to continue to love her until I take my very last breath. Hate me. Demote me. Whatever you need to do, but know I will never stop loving Tallie. Nothing but death will keep me from her.'

And tonight that had been too close to the truth. Not knowing where my mate was and not knowing if she was safe or even alive is not something I ever want to live with again. I need the connection all mates have to finally give me a peace of mind.

I expect Rip to yell. To punch me or make me beg for his blessing. I'm a proud man, but if Rip asks me to get on my knees and beg him for his approval, I would fucking do it. Anything to make Tallie mine.

Something I should have done a long time ago.

The silence stretches between us. I watch different emotions play across Rip's face. Dread continues to grow inside me and for a second, I think Rip will deny our bond. Why else would he not break the silence between us?

Not able to handle the unknown anymore, I try to break it. "Rip, I—"

"I've heard enough." He puts up a hand and my entire body tenses. My wolf rages inside of me, thinking that we'll be denied our mate. I don't want to fight Rip. He's the closest thing I've had of a brother, but I will if I have to.

"Everything I have done for Tallie has been to keep her safe. You know how much she and Imelda mean to me."

I nod. Rip's parents died at a young age. His aunt took him in and raised him as her own. I know he feels the need to repay them for everything they have done for him.

"But perhaps in my need to protect her, I have also denied her a chance at happiness." Rip's words stop me cold. I'm not entirely sure I hear them correctly.

"What are you saying?" I ask.

Now it's Rip's turn to sigh. He doesn't look mad—he doesn't look happy either—but there's a certain acceptance in his demeanor that wasn't there before.

"You shouldn't have kept this from me. Neither of you, but especially you. I understand why you did, though. I haven't been the most approachable with this topic," he says and I scoff.

Rip narrows his eyes at me. "Don't push me Alpha," he warns and since I've already pushed my luck too much tonight, I nod.

"What I'm saying," he continues, "is if you hurt Tallie, there will be nowhere you can hide that I won't find you. Break her heart and I will make sure you don't live to see another day."

Even though Rip threatened my life, I can't hide the smile on my face. "We have your blessing?"

"Yeah, you fucker, you have my blessing. If anyone is worthy enough for my cousin, I suppose it's you."

It's not exactly a glowing stamp of approval, but it's approval all the same. "Thank you, Rip." Those words are so insignificant to what I'm truly feeling. Nothing can capture the gratitude I feel and the new hope for my future.

One I will build with Tallie.

"Now grab a seat. You'll be the last to see Tallie once she wakes up. Imelda gets to see her daughter first and then I wish to speak with her. Alone." Rip sinks into the chair by the fire, so I occupy the one opposite him.

"That's fine. I can wait a little longer to see her." Now that she is going to be my forever.

The two of us fall into a comfortable silence, waiting for Tallie to stir.

CHAPTER 9
TALLIE

A warm towel presses against my forehead and someone hums a soothing tune. I'm awake, but I'm not ready to make that fact known yet. My body aches and there's a chill I can't quite shake. Another blanket would be ideal.

The events from earlier slowly play out in my head like my own personal movie. Thorne. An unfamiliar Omega. Pure heartache. Falling.

My paws slipped on a wet patch of grass and I frantically tried to dig my claws into the damp earth below me. Clearly I had been unsuccessful and now both my head and leg are throbbing.

Still, the pain is mild compared to the emptiness in my chest.

"I know you're awake, darling," my mom's soothing voice fills the room. She dabs at the sensitive spot on my head and my body jerks. "Enough of that. You'll let me tend to your wound."

I have no other choice but to obey. My mom is silent

as she washes off what I assume to be blood on my forehead. She mumbles something about it being a surface wound, so at least it's not that serious of an injury.

My leg on the other hand...

"Broken," my mom says as if reading my thoughts. "The healer just left and says you need to stay off your leg for the next week so your body has time to heal. You should be good as new then."

Wolves tend to heal quickly from injuries, but a broken bone will take longer.

"He also left pain medication in case you need it." My mom pulls back and I allow my eyelids to flutter open. The room is dimly lit by a fire and moonlight filters in through the window. My mom is the only person in the room with me, but I remember Thorne picking me up. He carried me home...but why?

"Thorne?" My voice cracks and my mom holds out a glass of water, which I gratefully take.

Ignoring my question, my mom sits at the edge of the bed, her hand resting on my non injured leg. "Tallie... what happened? When Thorne brought you home all muddy with blood...I thought the worst. Rip has been talking about rogues and..."

Her voice drifts off. The lighting is poor in the room, but I see her dab at her eyes, presumably wiping away tears.

I hate seeing my mother cry. She's one of the strongest women I know and for her to shed tears means she must have been beside herself with worry.

"It wasn't rogues, mom, or Nephilim," I say.

She lets out an audible sigh of relief. It's a small

comfort, but comfort nonetheless. "Then did something happen between you and Thorne? His eyes were blown wide when he brought you home. I've never seen him so worried."

"He's probably worried about getting back to his omega." I can't keep the bitterness out of my tone when I say it. My eyes start to sting with unshed tears, but if I start crying again, I'll never stop.

Not mating Daven had hurt, but that pain is nothing compared to what I'm feeling now. This is the pain that Rip is trying to keep me safe from. The all consuming void that threatens to overcome me.

"Omega? *What* omega?" Confusion etches my mom's features. As much as I don't wish to relive the moment, a small part of me wants for her to tell me she can fix everything. It's a childlike notion and completely impossible. And yet I still hope.

The words begin to tumble out of me. I tell her about the excitement I felt going over to Thorne's. How he didn't answer the door. Seeing he wasn't alone and realizing he was speaking to someone else. The hug they shared. And how I lost my ability to think straight. I let my wolf take over and we ran. We ran as hard and as far as our legs could carry us until we slipped and crashed to the bottom of the forest.

I'm sobbing by the end of it and somehow made it into my mom's arms. She rubs my back soothingly, promising everything is going to be okay, that we will figure this out and work through it together.

I don't know how long we stay in each other's arms, minutes, hours, but soon there is a faint knock on the door. My heart skips a beat as I push myself up, but it quickly deflates when Rip enters my bedroom.

My cousin looks drained. The dark circles under his eyes are more pronounced and he's still in the same clothes from this morning. He holds his tension in his shoulders, flexing and unflexing his arms as if trying to alleviate his sore muscles.

When Rip meets my gaze, his features soften. He gives me what might pass as a smile and I return it. Our alpha should be in bed asleep, but instead he's dealing with my stupidity. Guilt washes over me like a cold shower.

"Rip, I'm sorry—"

Rip silences me with his hand. He crosses my small room, and sits in the pink cushioned chair in the corner. It's almost comical to watch Rip fit his large body in the chair. He manages it somehow, and I repress a smile.

"You better not break my chair," I threaten.

A genuine smile flashes across his lips. "Then maybe you shouldn't have chairs that look as if they belong in the pack's nursery."

It is a small chair, but my room isn't huge. The bed takes up most of the room and I wanted to make myself a small nook for when I read or stitch up clothing from the nursery. Thorne had helped me find a chair and he set it up in my room for me.

My smile fades.

No one speaks for a moment. It's my mother who breaks the silence as she gets up and smooths down the skirt of her dress. "You two have much to discuss. I'm going to put on a pot of coffee." With that, she leans down and kisses my forehead and does the same to Rip before she leaves the room, closing the door behind her.

The room is once again quiet, just the sound of our breathing and the crackling of the fire surrounds us. Despite the heat, I still feel a chill—or maybe this is vulnerability—and I pull the blankets tighter around me.

I'm prepared for the verbal lashing I'm sure Rip has planned for me. Ready to hear how reckless I was. How I let my emotions drive me insead of my instincts.

But he does neither of those things. Instead, he says something much worse. "Thorne told me everything."

I didn't think I could be caught unawares again, but Rip proves me wrong. I should probably say something, but what is there to say that Thorne hasn't already said? So, instead of dredging up our relationship and letting panic take over, I say, "Did you kill him?" It's a sorry excuse for a joke and falls flat.

"I thought about it. But what kind of example would that set for others? I can't go around killing every guy that looks at you with impure thoughts." He sounds bitter about it. Typical alpha male.

"But I only thought about killing him," he says as if that's much better. I suppose it is. "He's downstairs waiting to see you."

"Thorne is here?" I squeak. My head swivels to the door as if he'd walk in after hearing his name. The door remains shut though. Do I want to see him? I'm not certain my heart can take it.

"He is. Quite distressed, actually. Said it's his fault you are injured. Apparently you saw him with an omega?"

As if I haven't relived that enough today, I nod. No point in lying. It's Rip and he knows me too well.

"I see. And you didn't think about asking him about the omega in his kitchen?"

My cheeks flush crimson. Of course I *thought* about it, but my wolf had been in control and she was heartbroken. She saw another person claiming what was hers, and it broke us. Indignation fills me as I say, "Sorry if I didn't want to hear about the person I love finding someone else."

"Yeah, well if you had, you would have learned that the only reason Omega Zora is at Thorne's is because I asked him to house her for the night."

The words are slow to register. I'm not certain I hear him correctly. "You...knew she was there?"

"I did. In fact, you might be able to relate to Omega Zora's story. Her father forbade her from seeing her alpha. Much like you, she didn't listen and continued to pursue a courtship. When her father found out, he kicked the girl out of his house. Called her all sorts of names, and even encouraged her brothers to berate her.

"Zora came into my home, completely beside herself. I agreed that her father's reaction was inappropriate and gave her my blessing to mate with her beloved. Unfortunately, he is out on patrol and won't be back until morning. I asked Thorne to house her until then, since she didn't seem to be comfortable around me."

Conflicting emotions battle to take center stage. Sadness for the poor omega. Guilt that I reacted without asking questions. Adoration and longing for Thorne. Embarrassment for myself.

"I'm sorry, Rip. I...I don't have an excuse for what I did, other than I love Thorne and it hurt to think I would lose another person to someone else. I should have asked questions."

"You should have," he agrees. "But I didn't come in here to patronize you. I came to apologize."

My mouth falls open. "*What*? You—apologize? For what?"

"For having you think you could not tell me about Thorne. None of this would have happened if you felt comfortable enough to approach me."

"Yeah, this would have been a lot easier if you weren't determined to refuse every non-beta male I tried to choose for myself," I snap. I can't help it, even though it's childish. If he had just understood earlier...

No. As easy as this would be for me to place all the blame on Rip, I can't ignore my part in all of this. I appreciated his apology but there's something else I want from him more. His trust in knowing I'm capable of making my own decisions.

Rip pushes himself up off the comically small chair and closes the distance between us. He is so damn tall I have to tilt my head up to get a good look at him.

My chubby-faced, playful cousin is still buried underneath the alpha who carries too much on his shoulders. He needs a partner to help alleviate the burden, but my cousin has never expressed interest in anyone for more than a week. There are plenty of women and men in town that would happily warm his bed for longer than a night, but Rip has built permanent walls around himself, shielding his heart from others.

I don't want to live like that.

I *can't* live like that.

Perhaps knowing this is what gave me the courage to say what I need to say next. "I appreciate your apology, Rip. You were only trying to save me from heartache, even if I couldn't see it at first. You've always been a good judge of character.

"However," I continue, "I also need you to trust me. Heartache is part of life, Rip. You can't shield me from that forever. I need to be able to make my own decisions when it comes to who I love."

"I know," he sighs, though he sounds far from happy about it. "I can't promise you I won't want to kill him a little bit when I see you together, knowing he's defiling my cousin."

A laugh bursts out of me and with it, tension I don't realize I'm holding on to. "Maybe it's me who is defiling your best friend."

Rip makes a face like he had just sucked on a sour lemon. "New rule. Let's not talk about you or him defiling anyone."

"You started it," comes my mature response.

I half expect Rip to stick his tongue out at me like he did when we were kids. He doesn't. Instead, he leans down and kisses my forehead before saying, "Just so we're clear, I approve."

How long have I wanted to hear those words? I wish it hadn't taken a broken leg to get here, but I can't blame my cousin for that. "Thank you," I whisper, hoping those two little words convey just how much his words and his approval mean to me. Not just as my Alpha King, but as my cousin.

Rip straightens himself up, all signs of his teasing demeanor gone, like they hadn't been there in the first place. I hope one day he finds someone that can bring that side out of him.

"I'll tell Thorne you're ready to see him. I'm sure you both have a lot to talk about." Rip offers me one last look, eyes scanning my body, down to my broken leg. "Stay off that. Bed for you."

"Yes, dad." I try not to roll my eyes, but fail.

With that, Rip leaves my room. Nerves begin to settle in, knowing what I have to do now.

I just hope it's not too late.

CHAPTER 10
THORNE

Each moment that ticks by agonizingly slowly is torture. I don't know how Tallie is and a storm brews inside me. I'm trying to respect her distance and the order from Rip to stay downstairs, but not even the Alpha King's order will keep me away from her for much longer.

My best friend has heard enough from me tonight, though.

I expected Rip to blow up when I came clean to him about everything, but my friend surprised me. I knew he was pissed though when I first carried Tallie in because his eyes darkened and flashed golden, meaning he was barely containing his wolf. He wanted to rip my throat out and I nearly let him.

It's shameful for an alpha to let his mate get hurt. We are supposed to protect them with our lives. Granted, I didn't plan for Tallie to walk in on me with Zora and jump to conclusions, but I should have been able to soothe her before she got hurt.

A broken leg, the healer said.

Which to a wolf, isn't a major injury, but it would still mean Tallie would need to stay in bed and rest until her leg heals. If there is one thing My Star hates the most, it's sitting and doing nothing.

She spends her days at the pack's nursery, caring for the babies and children while their parents are at work or need time to themselves. Tallie is so good with the pups and they flock to her like little sheep. Being away from them for a few days will be difficult, but I hope she listens to the doctor and rests. I will make certain she does.

Movement from down the hall has me springing to my feet. I know it's Rip because Imelda left Tallie's room a while ago to make coffee. She brought me a mug, but it sits untouched on the side table. I don't need coffee to wake up, my body is already buzzing with energy.

Rip barely makes it into the living room before I'm standing in front of him. Unlike most people, Rip doesn't shrink away from me due to my size. I'm large, even for an alpha. Rip is built similarly and stands at the same height as me. We make the perfect duo, not just with our height, but with the decisions we make. He's the protector and I'm the strategist.

It's always just *worked*.

Being at odds with him now fucking sucks, but there's little I can do to repair the damage until I know Tallie is safe.

"She's asking for you," Rip says and clasps my shoulder. Probably with more force than necessary. A weaker male would flinch, but I meet his stare head on.

"This is the part where I'm reminding you again that if you hurt her, I'll kill you, but I think you already know that. So instead I'll say, make her happy. And if I ever walk in on you two having sex, I'll rip your dick off."

The tension building between us disappears until it's almost gone. There will always be a lingering apprehension because I'm in love with his cousin and he wants what's best for her. I can respect that.

"Noted, alpha. Though I would prefer to never again think about your hands being anywhere near my dick—no offense," I smirk.

Rip scoffs. "You'd only be so lucky," he teases and loosens his hold on me. "Don't fuck this up again." He moves past me, presumably to find Imelda. Then hopefully home so he can get some much needed rest.

I'm at Tallie's door in seconds. I knock before coming in. I'm greeted with the smell of vanilla and burning wood. Tallie is sitting up in bed, a pillow behind her to prop her up. I take her in. The way the moonlight shines on her brown skin. The messy curls piled high on her head. Her mother must have changed her, since she's in a pink nightgown. My eyes travel down her body to her leg.

The healer bandaged her up well. I remember the blood I found on her forehead and notice it has been cleaned off. The tension I'm holding in my shoulder eases now that I can see her with my own eyes and know she's okay.

"Tallie, my love, you scared me. You scared all of us."

She has the decency to look embarrassed, but I'm not trying to scold her. I'm sure Rip did enough of that.

"Can I sit?" I gesture to the spot on the bed next to her.

When she nods, I take my spot next to her. The bed creaks under my weight and she wiggles out of the way to allow me more room.

"I'm sorry."

"I'm sorry."

We both speak at the same time, a smile playing on those beautiful red lips. "Let me go first," she says and I nod.

Tallie sucks in a deep breath and reaches for my hand. I take it as a good sign she wants me this close and is still willing to touch me.

"Rip told me why the omega is at your house. The horrors poor Zora had to go through, and you were offering her a place of safety. I didn't stop to ask. Instead, I jumped to conclusions—"

"I don't blame you for that. I'm sorry too. I should have told you; I know how it looked, but bringing her to my home was a last minute call. I know Rip has told you for the past few years that alphas will leave you for an omega, but you must realize, that's *not* going to happen to us. Never. I will not leave you."

"I know," Tallie smiles gently. A few stubborn tears roll down her cheeks, but I'm quick to wipe them away. "And I should have trusted you. I'm so, so sorry, my love. I understand if you don't forgive me—"

And that's where I silence her. My mouth is on hers, muffling her words. A cute gasp leaves her mouth, but then her soft lips are kissing me back. I take her head between my hands, keeping her right where I want her.

A growl leaves my throat. I want her. I want to dominate her and assure her everything is fine. That *we* are fine. But that would go against the healer's instructions, and I'm not willing to risk causing her further injury.

Reluctantly I break our kiss, even though Tallie whines and tries to pull me back. "You're injured, My Star. We can't get carried away." I remind.

Tallie looks like she's going to protest, but instead she pushes her bottom lip out in a cute pout before nodding.

"Don't be too disappointed. We have this time to plan our mating ceremony. Since you'll be adding two more people to that list."

That puts a smile on my beta's face. "You really want to mate me? Are you certain?"

"I have half a mind to take you over my knee and spank you until you realize just how *certain* I am," I growl.

Tallie bites her lip and I want nothing more than to kiss her again, pulling her bottom lip in my mouth to suck.

"Well, that doesn't sound too bad. I need to *really* believe it after all." Her eyes have a wicked gleam to them.

"Naughty girl. No spankings. We'll save that for the chase."

Where I'll chase my beta through the woods and claim her as mine once I find her. It's a game of cat and mouse I can't wait to play.

"Will you stay with me tonight? Now that everyone knows, I don't think anyone would mind," Tallie asks.

She's probably right. Her mother shared her approval with me and repeatedly thanked me for finding her daughter and bringing her home. No one would fault us spending the night together.

"Only if you promise to behave," I say, moving to situate myself next to her.

"But being naughty is so much more fun."

I growl, causing Tallie to laugh. She leans her head against my chest and my arms snake around her. "I'll be good. Just don't leave."

"I don't plan to," I say and pull the blankets around her.

Tallie relaxes against me and she struggles to keep her eyes open. My beta needs her sleep. "Good," she whispers and soon her breathing evens out, telling me she's fallen asleep.

I make good on my promise and hold her throughout the entire night.

CHAPTER II
TALLIE

One Week Later

My heart beats wildly in the still night. Faint howls carry in the wind, as anticipation begins to build. Some of us have been found, probably giving into their mate easily so as to not prolong the experience.

But not me. I like the chase too much and I know he does too.

Movement from my right has me sprinting in the opposite direction, forcing my legs to carry me as fast as they can. My broken leg—now healed—gives me some trouble, but it's easy to ignore with the adrenaline pumping through my veins.

Another howl. Another mate found.

Am I the last?

I'm reaching the boundary Rip set for the mating

couples, deeming this part of the forest safe from rogues and Nephilim, two things I'm not thinking about tonight.

There's only *him*.

I make an abrupt left turn, winding my body through the trees. My wolf pants, but refuses to slow down. She's excited to be claimed by her wolf and half tempted to stop running so he will find us faster.

The thought lingers in my mind a second longer before I push it away, breaking through a clearing in the trees. I slow my pace, wondering which direction to take now. I smell a couple to the right of me and hear their frantic mating. If I were in my human body, a blush would creep up my neck and to my cheeks.

I choose to run to the left for obvious reasons, but my brief hesitation costs me. I hear him before I can see him. Leaves crinkle under his paws, and branches snap. Charcoal gray fur peaks through the trees before a large dire wolf breaks through the clearing.

Excitement and fear wrestle for control and an involuntary whine leaves my wolf. The dire wolf huffs. I swear he's laughing at me. Thorne's dire wolf towers over me, the hard muscles of his body both extremely alluring and frightening.

I don't shy away from him though, despite that fact. I brazenly approach him, my smaller wolf rubs against his flank, scenting him. He growls low from the back of his throat, but I ignore his warning and do the same thing to his other side.

My wolf preens, happy to have scented her wolf.

I don't get to bask in my victory for long before my Alpha attacks.

He pounces, rolling his bulky body on top of mine. He's careful not to put too much of his weight on me. Thorne shifts on top, dark eyes fill with lust. "Shift, Beta," he commands.

For half a second I plan on not doing as I'm told to get a reaction out of him. But my need and desperation for Thorne is too strong to ignore and I shift underneath him.

The chill of the winter air caresses my naked human form. It barely phases me. An inferno builds inside my body, knowing Thorne is about to claim me. Once he does, we will be bonded for life.

Thorne ruts against me and I groan. "Baby..." the whine leaves my lips before I can stop it and the scent of my arousal permeates the air around us.

"*Fuck*, Tallie," Thorne growls, not as unaffected as he looks to be. Pride surges through me knowing how wound up my alpha is for me. Judging by the strain in his arm muscles and the hardness of his thick cock rutting between my legs, he's already halfway to a frenzy.

"Take me," I growl. The howls of the other mates surround us and I want to join them all in ecstasy. I need to be pulled apart and sewn back together. Stronger. Better.

"Hold on tight, My Star." I do as I'm told, winding my arms around his neck and my legs around his torso. I mold my body to his, needing the friction and heat of his body.

Without further warning, Thorne thrusts into me.

He's so big, I feel him so deeply inside of me. My eyes close, gold and white exploding behind my lids.

This feels different than every time before. It's more intense, more demanding, more needy. Just *more.*

He moves our bodies as one and I don't even mind the debris poking at my back. I can do little more than take his cock and moan sounds of my pleasure.

I groan, but it gets swallowed up by Thorne's searing kiss. Teeth and tongue clash for dominance, but Thorne wins out in the end. He claims my mouth, his tongue mingling with mine. He sucks my bottom lip into his mouth and we moan in unison.

His thrusts grow more frenzied. My need for him grows more chaotic. I want him to bite me. To leave his mark on my neck that will allow everyone to know that I'm his. That we won't be a secret anymore.

I've only ever planned mating ceremonies. I never could quite understand why the mates stayed out most of the night and now I do. Pulling away from him now would be impossible.

He breaks the kiss and I gasp for air. Thorne's lips trail down my neck, to my chest. He kisses every part of me, nipping and sucking.

It's all too much.

But not enough.

I run my hands down his back, my nails digging into him in the process. He growls, and flexes his back muscles.

What a sight my alpha must be now. Gorgeous dark skin shining under the moonlight. Strong thighs flexing each time he thrusts forward.

"You. Are. Mine." He punctuates each word with a thrust. My body jerks and I cry out in pleasure. I may feel embarrassed about my needy sounds later, but at the moment it's all I'm capable of.

My words are slow to come to me, but I manage to pant out, "Claim me, alpha. Make me yours for the world to see."

His hold on me tightens and he draws me into his arms. He sits back on his haunches, straightening his back. I straddle him, using his shoulders as leverage.

"Ride me." He doesn't ask, he commands. Stubborn alpha.

I move my body up and down on his cock. From this position, I feel so much more and I know it won't be much longer until I come undone.

"Thorne...Alpha, *please*." I beg of him.

Thorne snatches up my hair in one of his hands, pulling it off to the side and away from my shoulder. I tilt my head, giving him perfect access to my unmarked neck.

His eyes flash golden once and then his mouth is on my shoulder, kissing and sucking. His teeth scrape across my skin and just when I'm about to beg him again, he sinks his fangs into my neck.

Red hot pain and pleasure overtake my body and I scream. A wall inside of me crumbles as love, adoration, lust, and happiness filter into my body. I sense him all around me as the bond snaps into place. It's the thing that tips me over the edge and I come so hard. He follows soon after, his knot forming inside of me, locking us together. It's a little painful, but I like it. Betas aren't as primed like omegas to take knots, but I have gotten used to Thorne's. I crave it now.

My body gives out and I fall on to his chest. He brings his strong arms up to wrap around me, keeping me close. Thorne's heart pounds rapidly in his chest, very similar to my own heart right now.

Through our newly formed bond, I feel his pride. The warmth of his love wraps around me like a fuzzy blanket. "I'm your mate." My voice sounds so soft.

"You're my mate," he agrees, kissing the top of my forehead. The bite on my shoulder is only a dull pain now, and in a few minutes I won't feel it at all.

The forest around us grows quiet. I no longer hear the howls of the other mates and I wonder if they are snuggled up and locked together like Thorne and me.

I can't help but to think back to the road that led us here. The secret nights we shared together. The way our bodies connected for the first time. The pain of thinking I lost him. All of it led us here and I wouldn't change it for the world.

"You're thinking too hard, mate."

Mate.

The world fills me with butterflies and I only hope they never go away.

"I'm thinking about us," I say, tilting my head up to look at him. His eyes hold so much love inside of them I almost start to cry. "About our life together. How happy I am."

"And what a life it will be," he hums, peppering my forehead with angel soft kisses.

I think of the life that awaits us. The home we will

grow our family together. My belly swollen with his pups. Growing old and surrounded by our grandchildren and, if we are lucky, our great-grandchildren.

That future starts *now*.

"Alpha?"

"Hmm?" he answers absentmindedly, playing with strands of my hair.

I place my hand on his chest, a devious smile on my lips. "I'm ready to take care of that knot now."

Without another word, Thorne lays me back on the ground and for the remainder of the night, he shows me just how perfect we are together.

Together as mates.

WANT MORE?

Want to receive bonus content and be the first to know about my books, signings, and ARC signups? Make sure to join my Newsletter.

Sign up for my newsletter here!

ALSO BY TATI B. ALVAREZ

Dawn Of Dasos

1. The Ambrosia Throne

2. The Ambrosia Deception

3. The Ambrosia War - *Coming Soon*

Grym Hollow

1. The Dragon's Rose

1.5 Tallie's Secret

2. The Wolf's Mate - Coming Soon

THANK YOU FOR READING!

I can't thank you enough for picking up my book. I hope you enjoyed it as much as I enjoyed writing it! If you did and are willing please consider leaving a review on your favorite book sites. This helps out small authors like me so much. Thank you for your continued support!

About the Author

Tati B. Alvarez lives in Austin, Texas with her family. She spends most days lost in her own head, creating stories. When she is not writing, you can find her vacationing at Disney World.

Made in the USA
Coppell, TX
02 April 2025